A Trap to Catch
Brer Rabbit

First published in Great Britain by HarperCollins Publishers Ltd in 1998

1 3 5 7 9 10 8 6 4 2

Copyright © 1998 Enid Blyton Company Ltd. Enid Blyton's signature
mark and the word 'TOYLAND' are Registered Trade Marks of Enid Blyton Ltd.
For further information on Enid Blyton please contact www.blyton.com

ISBN: 0 00 664674-3

Printed and bound in Belgium.

Enid Blyton™

TOYLAND™ STORIES

A Trap to Catch Brer Rabbit

Collins

An Imprint of HarperCollins*Publishers*

One day, Brer Fox, Brer Bear and Brer Wolf were talking about all the tricks that old Brer Rabbit had played on them.

"Once he made Brer Terrapin crawl down a hole," said Brer Fox. "Then he told me that there was treasure in that hole. When I put my paw down to get the treasure, Brer Terrapin bit me and wouldn't let go. It was scary, I can tell you."

"Let's play the same trick on old Brer Rabbit," said Brer Bear. "We can pretend there is a sack of gold down a hole.

Then Brer Fox can hide down there and catch Brer Rabbit when he goes after the gold."

"But Brer Rabbit is very clever," said Brer Wolf, "so we'll have to make our plans carefully. Listen." And Brer Wolf explained his plan.

First, they would all whisper together in a corner whenever Brer Rabbit came by to make him think they had some big secret.

Then they would let Brer Rabbit see them dragging along a heavy sack. And then they would tell the tattling Jack Sparrow that they had hidden a sack of gold down the hole near Brer Rabbit's house.

"We'll ask Jack Sparrow *not* to tell Brer Rabbit," said Brer Fox. "Then, he'll go straight to old Brer Rabbit. He always does."

"Brer Fox," said Brer Wolf. "When Brer Rabbit comes along to steal the gold, you be ready to grab him. Then bring him to my house and we'll put him in the pot and eat him up."

It seemed a very good plan. After all, Brer Rabbit had tricked them often enough.

During the next few days, wherever Brer Rabbit went, he came across Brer Wolf, Brer Fox and Brer Bear whispering together.

"What's this?" he asked. But the other animals did not reply. "Well, keep your secret to yourself," cried Brer Rabbit. "See if I care."

Then one day, Brer Rabbit caught sight of the three animals dragging a heavy sack. A clinking noise came from it because the sack was full of old tins.

"What's that?" asked Brer Rabbit.

"Mind your own business," said Brer Wolf, trying to hide the sack behind him.

"You three *are* behaving strangely," said Brer Rabbit.

Next day, the tattling Jack Sparrow flew down beside Brer Rabbit.

"Heyo," he said. "I've some news for you."

"Go away," said Brer Rabbit. "You're a chatterbox."

"Ah, but this is great news," said Jack Sparrow, hopping about with excitement. "Brer Wolf told me, and he told me not to tell you, Brer Rabbit. Brer Wolf, Brer Fox and Brer Bear have a sack of gold and they are hiding it down that hole over there, to stop you stealing it."

"I don't believe you," said Brer Rabbit. "Brer Wolf wouldn't tell you a secret like that, Jack Sparrow."

Jack Sparrow flew off, chattering with rage.
"Now why should Brer Wolf tell
Jack Sparrow that?" Brer Rabbit
wondered. "Why should he
make up such a silly story?
And what's all this whispering
and dragging about of sacks?"

That night, Brer Rabbit crept quietly out of his house. He hid near the hole and kept watch until morning.

No one had come near the hole so Brer Rabbit went to take a look. The grass was not flattened down at all and it didn't seem as if anyone had been dragging sacks up to it. But there were footprints there. Brer Rabbit bent down to look at them.

"These are Brer Fox's footprints!" he thought scratching his head. He lay down very quietly beside the hole and listened. Someone was breathing down there.

"Hmmmmm!" said Brer Rabbit to himself. "First time I ever knew a sack of gold that could breathe – or one that smelt like that either. Seems to me it's all a silly trick. Brer Fox is down there – and he's waiting for me to put down my paw to get a sack that isn't there. Well, I'll just trick him instead!"

Brer Rabbit fetched a spade and began to fill in the hole with earth as fast as he could.

When Brer Fox saw that he was being buried, he yelled out in fear. "Is that you, Brer Wolf? What are you doing?"

"It's me, Brer Rabbit," said Brer Rabbit, pretending to be astonished. "Why, Brer Fox, what are you doing down there? Jack Sparrow told me Brer Wolf had put a sack of gold down this hole – so I've come along to fill it in, in case anyone else gets to know of it, and robs poor old Brer Wolf."

"You let me out!" yelled Brer Fox.

"Certainly not," said Brer Rabbit. "I think you're after the gold, and I'm going to bury you and fetch Brer Wolf along! And I'm going to get a reward for saving his gold."

"There isn't any gold!" shouted Brer Fox, as more earth and stones came rattling down on top of him.

"You can tell me what you like," said Brer Rabbit, enjoying himself. "But I don't believe you."

He buried Brer Fox and went off to knock on Brer Wolf's door. Brer Wolf and Brer Bear were waiting for Brer Fox to come along with Brer Rabbit.

But when Brer Wolf opened the door, it was Brer Rabbit who stood there, grinning.

"Heyo, Brer Wolf," he said. "I've some news for you. That tattling Jack Sparrow told me you'd hidden a sack of gold down the hole near my house, so this morning I went along with a spade to fill in the hole in case a thief found your gold and stole it."

"Very kind of you," said Brer Bear, looking sour.

"Well, Brer Bear, there *was* a thief down there," said Brer Rabbit. "After your gold, I guess. So I buried him, and came to fetch you."

"Buried him!" said Brer Bear, in a fright. "Why, that was old Brer Fox!"

"How did you know?" said Brer Rabbit. "Well, I thought I'd just come and tell you. Goodbye!"

He slipped round the side of the house and saw Brer Wolf and Brer Bear setting off with spades, to rescue Brer Fox.

Brer Rabbit slipped into Brer Wolf's house. He took a basket and filled it with carrots, onions and cabbages. Then he left a note on the table.

"Dear Brer Wolf," said the note. "I guess I deserve a reward for saving your gold from a thief. I'm taking carrots, onions and cabbages. Thanks very much."

Off he skipped with the basket...

...and you should have seen Brer Wolf's face that night when he came back tired out with digging up poor Brer Fox. "Look at that note!" he said to Brer Bear, in a rage. "What's the good of playing tricks on Brer Rabbit? All he does is to use our trick to play a joke on us! And now we've nothing for supper, because he's taken all the vegetables!"

And that's what comes of trying to trap old Brer Rabbit!

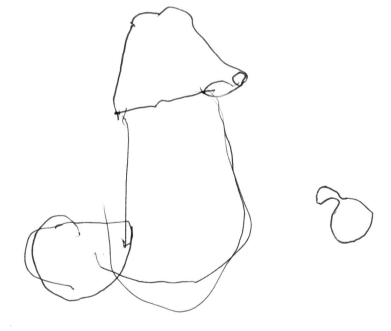